Snake Hair

Written by Zoë Clarke

Illustrated by Vladimir Aleksic

Long ago, there was a young man called Perseus.

Perseus's mother, Danae, was very beautiful, and the king wanted to marry her.

But Danae didn't want to marry the king.

When the king asked again, Perseus said, "My mother will never marry you!"

The king thought he'd be able to make Danae marry him if her son wasn't around. So he came up with a way to get rid of Perseus.

He asked everyone to bring him a gift.

"Anyone who doesn't bring me a gift will be set a task," he said.

The king knew Perseus was too poor to bring anything, and he planned to give him a task so difficult he wouldn't ever come back.

Perseus didn't have anything for the king, so he waited to see what task he'd be given.

The king smiled.

"I want you to get me the head of Medusa!"

Everyone gasped. Medusa was a monster with hair made of snakes – and anyone who looked at her would turn to stone.

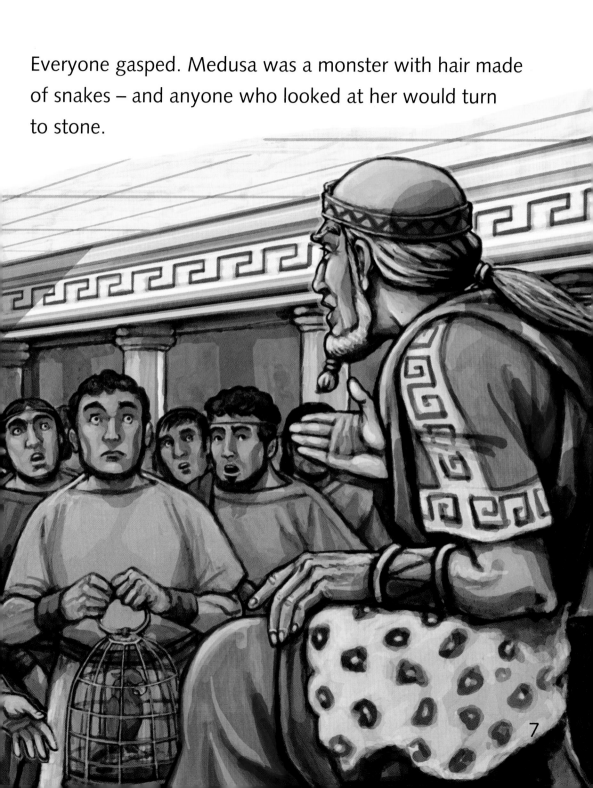

Perseus realised he'd been tricked,
but he didn't want to look weak.

"I'll get you Medusa's head!" he said.

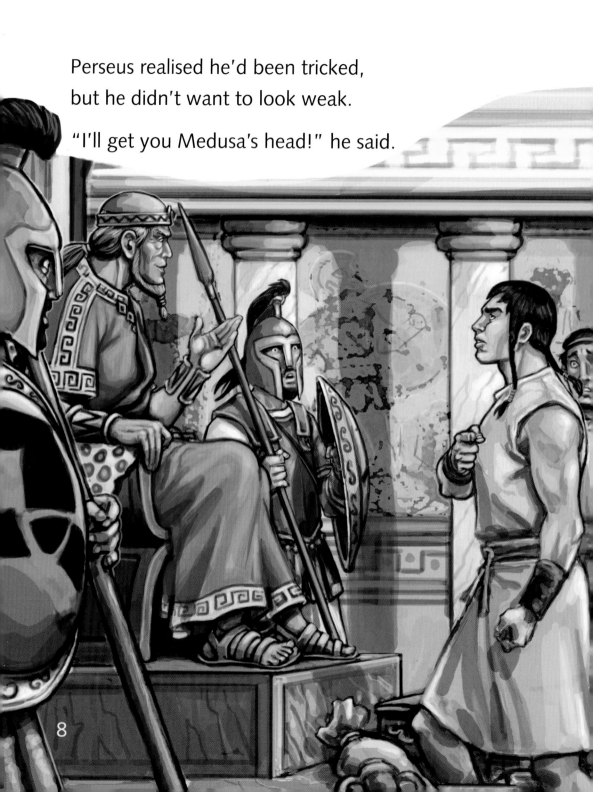

Two gods gave Perseus a shiny shield and a sharp sword.

They told him where to find three sisters who knew where Medusa was. He'd recognise them, because they shared one eye between them.

Perseus sailed away from home, and found the island where the three sisters lived.

They refused to help, so Perseus stole their eye.

"I'll give back your eye if you tell me where to find Medusa."

They told him where Medusa was, but laughed, "You won't come back alive!"

Perseus sailed through storms for
many days, until he reached
the island where Medusa lived.

He climbed up a rocky
cliff and crept into
a dark cave.

The cave was cold and slimy, and Perseus could hear snakes hissing in the dark.

He shivered. How was he going to cut off Medusa's head without looking at her?

Then he had an idea. His shield was so shiny it was like a mirror. If he held it up, he'd see Medusa's reflection in it.

Perseus held up his shield, and waited.

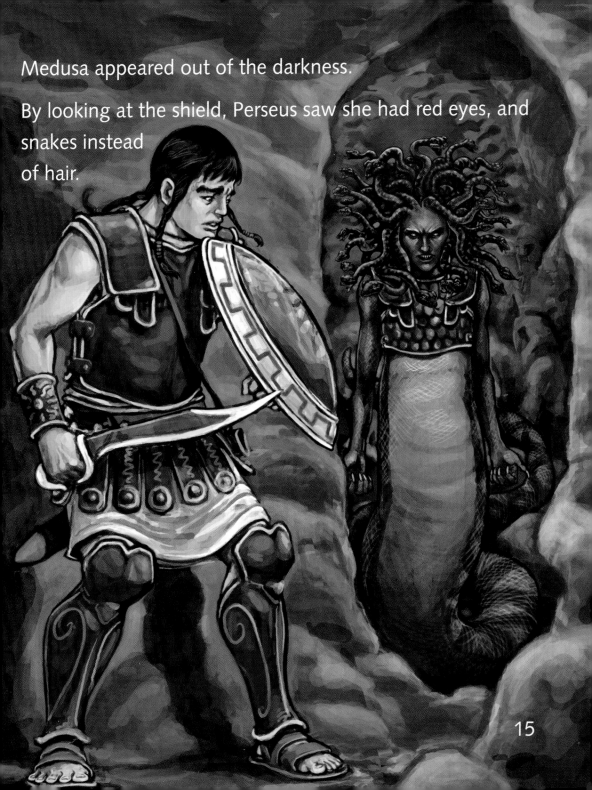

Medusa appeared out of the darkness.

By looking at the shield, Perseus saw she had red eyes, and snakes instead
of hair.

Medusa looked around the cave.

"I smell a human!" she hissed.

16

Perseus's hands began to shake, but he held his shield up high.

Medusa came closer and closer.

Perseus kept his eyes on his shield.

Suddenly, Perseus swung his sword, and cut off her head with one stroke!

He grabbed Medusa's snake hair, and put her head into a bag. The snakes hissed angrily as he carried the bag out of the cave.

When Perseus returned home, he went straight to the king and opened the bag.

"I have the head of Medusa!"

The king cried "No!" but it was too late. He looked at Medusa's eyes, and in a flash he was turned to stone.

Perseus smiled. He'd saved his mother from the king – but he kept Medusa's head, just in case he ever needed it again.

The king's plan

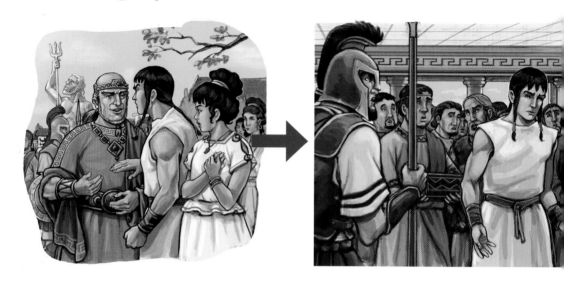

Perseus's plan

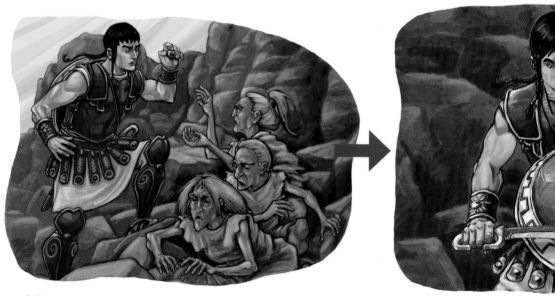

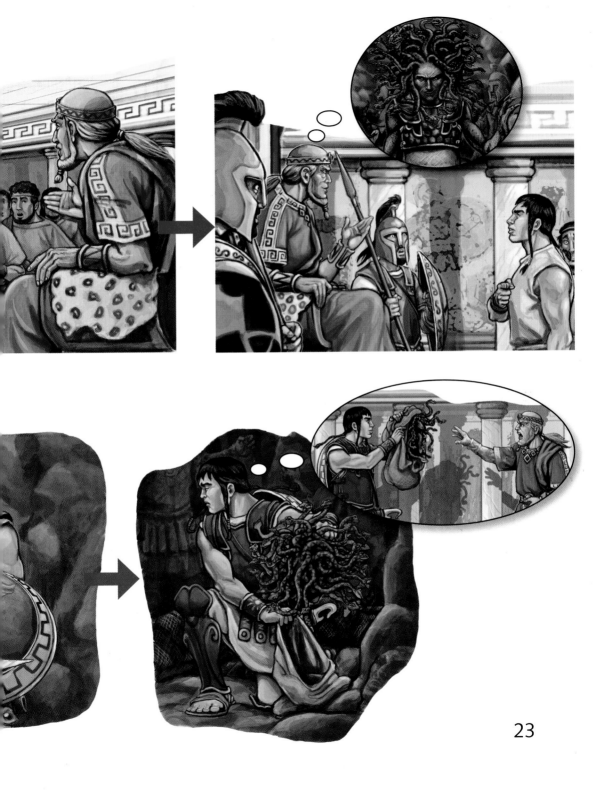

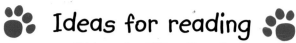

Ideas for reading

Written by Gillian Howell
Primary Literacy Consultant

Learning objectives: *(reading objectives correspond with Turquoise band; all other objectives correspond with Ruby band)* read independently and with increasing fluency longer and less familiar texts; know how to tackle unfamiliar words that are not completely decodable; understand underlying themes, causes and points of view; improvise using a range of drama strategies and conventions to explore themes such as hopes, fears and desires

Curriculum links: History, Citizenship

Interest words: shield, sword, recognise, island, slimy, mirror, reflection

Resources: pens and paper, collage materials

Word count: 525

Getting started

- Read the title together and look at the illustration. Check the children can see that the woman has snakes for hair and ask if anyone has heard of a story with a character like this.

- Turn to the back cover and read the blurb together. Ask the children if they know who Perseus is and explain that he was a character in Ancient Greek myths. Ensure they understand what a myth is.

- Turn to pp2–3 and ask the children to find the names of the two characters. Help them to pronounce the names.

Reading and responding

- Read pp2–3 together and ask children to predict how the king will react to Perseus's statement.

- Remind the children to use their knowledge of phonics and familiar spelling patterns to help them work out new words.

- As they are reading, ask the children to find out who the monster with snake hair is, what task Perseus has to perform and how he does it.